stars in
your eyes

stars in your eyes

stories chosen by
wendy cooling

A Dolphin Paperback

First published in Great Britain in 1997
by Orion Children's Books
a division of the Orion Publishing Group Ltd
Orion House
5 Upper St Martin's Lane
London WC2H 9EA

A catalogue record for this book is available
from the British Library
Typeset by Deltatype Ltd,
Birkenhead, Merseyside
Printed in Great Britain
ISBN 1 85881 463 4

contents

stage fright

jean ure

No! Natalie! Stop!'

Natalie stopped. She came forward to the edge of the stage. *Now* what was the matter?

'What's happening?' said Miss Frazer. 'I'm not getting anything from you!'

Natalie bristled. What did she mean, she wasn't getting anything? Natalie had been raging and screaming at the very top of her voice!

'This girl,' said Miss Frazer, 'Gretchen … she's in a blazing temper. Right?'

'Yes.' And when you were in a blazing temper you raged and screamed. At least, Natalie did.

'The question we have to ask ourselves,' said Miss Frazer, 'is *why* is she in a blazing temper?'

Natalie mumbled, 'Because she's scared.'

Not just scared: terrified. Terrified because it was war time and while she was safe in England her mum and dad were still in Germany. They had already been through all this!

'You're petrified with fear,' said Miss Frazer, 'in case your parents are killed. Your parents are Jewish, and we all know what the Nazis did to the Jews. And it's *because* you're so scared that you take it out on everyone around you. All the people who are trying to help you. You're too strong a person to sit down and weep. So you shout, you rage – '

Which was exactly what she had been doing. So what was Miss Frazer's stupid problem?

'I'll tell you what the problem is,' said Miss Frazer. 'All I'm getting from you is anger. Anyone can give me anger! Anger is one of the easiest emotions to put across. It doesn't cost you a thing.'

I beg your *pardon*, thought Natalie, indignant. It took a lot of energy, being angry did.

'Oh, it's all very splendid, all this ranting and raging! But there's nothing behind it. It's empty! Just Natalie Rogers putting on an act. Showing off, in other words. Well, let me tell you,' said Miss Frazer, 'I am not interested in people showing off, and neither will the judges be. Showing off is not the way we win cups for drama. The way we win cups for drama is by portraying genuine, heartfelt emotions. Go back and do it again! We'll take it from the top. And this time, please remember … I want to feel the fear behind that rage!'

Natalie turned, simmering, and stomped back up stage. How were you supposed to show two emotions at once? It wasn't fair! No one could do it. If they'd been acting the whole play, the audience would have *known* she was frightened. But all they were doing was just one short scene. Her and Ros Taylor, and it was easier for Ros. She was playing an English girl. Natalie had to pretend to be German and speak with a German accent. *And* to be angry and frightened at the same time. It just wasn't possible!

Twice more Miss Frazer made them stop and go back to the beginning. Each time she yelled at Natalie for not giving.

'You're not giving me a thing! It's all show! I want real emotion!'

At the end of the rehearsal she gave them their notes. To Ros she said, 'It's shaped up very nicely, Ros. You'll do just fine.'

To Natalie she said, 'I'm sorry, but you're still holding back, Natalie. You really must try to open those floodgates.'

'Floodgates!' Natalie kicked viciously at a tin can as she walked to the bus stop with Ros. 'What's she on about? Floodgates?'

Rather timidly Ros said, 'I think she meant you've got to open up.'

'*Open up*?'

Natalie glared. Hastily, Ros retreated.

'It isn't anything personal. She's always having a go at people. She went on at Diane Colby so much she made her cry.'

Natalie tossed her head. 'She's not going to make me cry!'

Nothing made Natalie cry. Natalie was tough. She swung her school bag – boff! – against a lamp post.

'Stupid cow! Hope she walks under a bus!'

'You'd better watch it,' advised Ros, 'or you'll walk under one yourself.'

'No way!' said Natalie. 'We're going to go to that Festival tomorrow and we're going to *win*. That'll show her!'

At nine o'clock next morning, all the members of Miss Frazer's special drama group gathered outside the school gates to wait for the coach that would take them to the Festival. The Festival was held every year at Stapeley Hall, a big house the other side of town. Miss Frazer's girls always did well. Last year they had won a silver medal for the Over 14s duologues, and the year before that a couple of bronzes. It was a while since they had actually won a gold. But this year, thought Natalie … this year she would show them!

The coach rolled up and they all climbed aboard. Everyone was there except Miss Frazer.

'Where's Miss Frazer?' asked Joanne Dixon, one of the senior girls.

'Fallen under a bus,' muttered Ros. She and Natalie both giggled.

'I'm afraid Miss Frazer can't be with us.' It was Mrs Dewey, the Head of English, who told them. 'She had a rather nasty accident on the way home last night.'

There was a shocked silence. Natalie had heard of people's blood running cold in their veins. It was what hers did, now. She could feel it, turning to ice, even as she sat there; draining from her cheeks, freezing her extremities, leaving her stiff and pale as a marble statue.

'Is she going to be all right?' said Joanne. She was talking about Miss Frazer, of course; not Natalie.

'We hope so,' said Mrs Dewey. 'We very much hope so. In the meantime, the best way to help her is for you to get out there and give it all you've got. I know she'll be thinking of you, so do your very best for her.'

Ros's hand came sneaking into Natalie's. She squeezed it, hard.

'It's just a coincidence,' she whispered. 'It wasn't your fault! You didn't make it happen. You can't make things happen just by thinking of them.'

Ros was right; you couldn't make things happen just by thinking of them. Goodness, if you could, the world would be in chaos!

The world was in chaos, but not because of people thinking things. Because of people doing things. Natalie hadn't done anything! It was like when she was little and her mum used to warn her not to pull nasty faces.

'Otherwise the wind will change and you'll be stuck like it.'

But Natalie hadn't given a fig and the wind never *had* changed. It was just a silly old wives' tale that mothers used to frighten their children.

'It wasn't anything to do with you.' Ros whispered it, urgently. 'It's just one of those things.'

'Yes,' said Natalie. 'I know.'

All the same, she couldn't help feeling wretched about it. Mrs Dewey glanced across at her and said, 'You're looking very peaky, Natalie! Are you all right?'

Natalie nodded.

'It's just nerves,' said Ros.

But Natalie Rogers never suffered from nerves. Other people might have panic attacks and feel sick and forget their lines. Not Natalie! Miss Frazer had once tried to comfort them by saying that you couldn't truly call yourself an actress until you'd had at least one bout of stage fright.

'Every actor or actress worth their salt has known the meaning of fear.'

Natalie didn't believe a word of it! It was just another old wives' tale, like the wind changing.

They reached Stapeley Hall and were taken into the Green Room. They had an hour to wait until it was their turn to go on. An hour of nail biting for some, but not for Natalie. Surely not for Natalie!

Ros slapped at Natalie's hand.

'Stop it! Chewing yourself.'

Natalie hadn't even realised she was doing it …

Other groups besides theirs were gathered in the Green Room. Mostly, they all kept to themselves, in the areas they had marked out as their territory. Some people did voice exercises – 'Oo-ah, ee-ah, ay-ah'. Some lay flat on their backs on the floor. Some sat white-faced and huddled. A few didn't seem affected at all.

'I think I'll go to the loo,' said Ros.

'I'll come with you,' said Natalie.

Five minutes later, Natalie was trotting off there again. And then again. And then a third time! The palms of her hands were moist and sticky, the sweat was trickling through her hair, she felt sick and almost as if she might faint. Was this what people called stage fright?

On her way back to the Green Room for the fourth time, she heard a voice call out to her.

'Natalie!'

She stopped, and turned. Miss Frazer!

'Natalie, I just wanted – '

'Miss Frazer, I'm r-really s-s – '

They spoke together. It was Natalie who broke off. How could you say to someone that you were sorry you had wished they would fall under a bus?

'I just wanted to wish you luck,' said Miss Frazer.

She looked pale. Pale as a marble statue. Pale as a lily. Almost transparent. But she was there!

'You must forgive me, Natalie, for being so harsh with you yesterday.' Her voice was a thin trail of sound. 'It was just that it was so frustrating … I knew you could do it! I *know* you can do it. I know you have it in you. But I ought not to have shouted. I was a bit upset because my little cat was in the vet and I – I wasn't sure whether she was going to come out … but that is no excuse! I don't believe you get the best from people by losing your temper. So please, Natalie – '

Miss Frazer held out both hands in a gesture of apology. Natalie stood, embarrassed, not knowing what to say. She had never had a grown up apologise to her before. And truth to tell, she wasn't sure that she deserved it. Maybe she hadn't tried as hard as she ought. Miss Frazer was quite right: anger was easy to act. Showing that you were scared was far more difficult.

'Just go on and do your best,' said Miss Frazer. 'That is as much as anyone can ask.'

'Natalie!'

Ros was calling to her from the Green Room. Natalie gave Miss Frazer a quick, rather lopsided grin – lopsided because her bottom lip was doing its best to smile whilst her top one would insist on trembling – and went racing back down the corridor. It was time to go on!

'My legs are like jelly,' whispered Ros.

'So are mine,' whispered Natalie.

And then they were out there, standing on stage, and there wasn't any time to think of their legs. They were Nora and Gretchen, and it was the Second World War.

Yesterday, at rehearsal, Natalie had concentrated on her rage. On being angry, and shouting and projecting her voice. Today she concentrated instead on the pain. The pain of being separated from her mum and dad, and the fear she felt that she might never see them again. She let the anger take care of itself.

At the end of the day, when the results were announced, Natalie Rogers and Rosalind Taylor of Leaminster High School were awarded the Gold Medal for the Under 14s duologues.

'We did it!' cried Ros. 'Or you did, actually,' she said, being generous. 'You played the main part.'

'Yes, but I couldn't have done it without you,' said Natalie. Or without Miss Frazer, she silently added.

As they boarded the coach to go home, it was Natalie, this time, who said. 'Where's Miss Frazer?'

Heads turned, from all over the coach, to look at her. Mrs Dewey, gently, said, 'Don't you remember, Natalie? Miss Frazer had an accident. She's in hospital.'

'She can't be!' said Natalie. 'She was here!'

There was a silence.

'I only wish she could have been,' said Mrs Dewey. 'She would have been so proud of you!'

But she spoke to me, thought Natalie. She spoke to me!

'I'll tell you what,' said Mrs Dewey. 'If she's well enough on Monday, I'm sure she'd love to have a visit from you. From both of you! Then she could tell you herself how proud she is. That would be nice, wouldn't it?'

Natalie smiled, dutifully. But to Ros, under her breath, she muttered: 'She *was* here. She wished me luck!'

'You must have been daydreaming,' said Ros, kindly. 'You know what you're like.'

On Monday morning, at first break, Mrs Dewey drove both girls to the hospital to pay their promised visit.

Miss Frazer was sitting up in bed against a mound of pillows. She looked quite cheerful though her head was bandaged and her face dark with bruises.

'Oh, dear!' she said. 'I am a sorry sight, aren't I? One broken leg, three cracked ribs, one split skull … I only recovered consciousness yesterday morning. I missed out on all the fun! And I was so looking forward to being there with you.'

Ros squeezed meaningfully at Natalie's arm.

'I felt that you were there,' said Natalie.

'I certainly was in spirit. I'm so cross with myself, I can't tell you! But that's enough about me. Sit down, both of you, and show me the good news.'

Eagerly, Ros and Natalie held out their medals.

'Congratulations!' cried Miss Frazer. 'Both of you! I knew you could do it, if you tried.'

'It was Natalie, really,' said Ros. 'She opened up the floodgates, like you said.'

Natalie's cheeks grew peony pink. She looked earnestly at Miss Frazer.

'I couldn't have done it without you,' she said.

Miss Frazer laughed, and pressed a hand to her ribs.

'Oh! I must remember not to do that. It hurts!'

'I'm really sorry,' said Natalie.

'Sorry? You have nothing to be sorry for! You should be feeling over the moon. I certainly am!'

Ten minutes later, as they stood up to go, Natalie suddenly thought of something. Shyly, she said, 'How is your cat?'

'My cat?' A smile lit Miss Frazer's face. 'She's well! She's back home. My mother's looking after her till I get out of hospital. Between you and me, I think it was because of her I had the accident ... I was so worried, and in such a rush to get to the vet, it made me careless. But all's well that ends well, as someone famous once said. Do you know who it was who said it?'

Ros and Natalie exchanged grins. This was more like Miss Frazer!

'William Shakespeare,' they chorused.

It wasn't until they were in Mrs Dewey's car, being driven back to school, that Ros said, 'How did you know about Miss Frazer's cat?'

'I don't know.' Natalie rumpled her brow, trying to remember. How had she known about Miss Frazer's cat?

She shook her head. 'Someone must have told me,' she said.

the shell house

jill parkin

Miranda lived in a tall green house at the top of a high, high cliff. Steep steps climbed up the cliff from the seashore, and a path led from the top of the cliff to Miranda's garden gate. And Miranda loved the sea. Her bedroom was right at the top of the tall green house. From one window she could see the long garden, and from the other she could see the pebbles and the waves. At night she fell asleep with the sound of the sea in her ears.

Every morning Miranda woke early to run down the stairs to the front door and then down the steps cut into the high cliff to the shore. And every morning she went past her favourite painting, which hung on the wall just outside her bedroom door. It was a beautiful young woman with long, dark, shiny hair, and eyes as deep blue as mussel shells. She sat on a rock, but instead of legs, she had a silvery, greeny-grey tail which glistened like a fish's tail. The mermaid was Miranda's grandmother, whom she had never known.

When Miranda reached the shore every morning, she walked here and there filling her pockets with shells. There were round curly dog whelk shells; dark blue mussel shells which were silvery inside; round, pointed limpet shells; long, thin razor shells; fan-shaped scallop shells, and the occasional oyster shell. She picked them out from among the pebbles and the seaweed. She even gathered broken pieces of shell, sometimes finding lovely colours: violet, yellow and mottled greys.

When her pockets were full, Miranda ran back up the steps in the high cliff towards the tall green house in time for breakfast. She sat at the table, and all the time she thought about the shells in her pockets, but she hardly ever talked about them.

Miranda would slip down from the table while her parents were reading their newspapers and run through the passage to the back door which led to the long, narrow garden. Beyond the herb border, it was a rather wild place. The grass was taller and taller the further down the garden Miranda ran. She even went past the shed, which was about as far as anyone else ever went. No one had been that way with a lawn mower for years, and Miranda pushed through grass which met over her head. Then she stopped.

There among the tall grasses, was a beautiful, tiny shell house, just the right size for a girl. The chimney was a stack of round, pointed limpet shells. The roof was made of white scallop shells, the door of dark blue mussel shells, and the walls of cockle shells of many different sizes. The door handle was a razor shell and the door knocker a curly dog-whelk shell. The windows were made of mother-of-pearl taken from the inside of oyster shells. A prettily coloured path leading to the house was made of broken pieces of shell. It was

Miranda's house, and she had made it all by herself. And nobody knew. Unless her grandmother the mermaid knew. Miranda thought she probably did.

One morning Miranda did not appear at breakfast. 'Where's Miranda?' they asked. Her father ran upstairs to Miranda's room and looked down at the seashore from her front window, but there was no sign of her. Then he looked down the long garden and he saw something glinting in the sunshine.

He ran with Miranda's mother past the shed which was as far as anyone ever went, through uncut grass which came up above their knees. And then they felt something underfoot. It was the beginning of the tiny shell path. At the end of the path, they saw it. Miranda's shell house.

For a minute they stood there looking. They had never seen anything like it. Her father opened the small door.

And there, curled up fast asleep, with a violet sea snail shell in her hand, was Miranda. Her mother gently shook her awake. 'Why, Miranda, whatever has been going on?' she said. And Miranda opened eyes as blue as mussel shells and smiled, and said: 'Mum, I've been dreaming all about Grandma.'

'I do wish,' said Miranda's grandmother in Miranda's dream, 'that your mother would show you the old sewing table in her room. When I was a little girl, I kept all my bits and pieces in that sewing table.'

'Your threads and scissors and things?' asked Miranda in her dream.

'Goodness me, no,' said Grandma. 'I wasn't that sort of girl. I preferred the seashore to sewing. Next time it's raining and you can't go out, ask your mother about Grandma's sewing table.'

And with a swish of her mermaid's tail, she was gone, back into the sea and out of Miranda's dream.

One day Miranda had a cold. She couldn't go out and she read stories in her bedroom until she couldn't read any more. She sneezed into her sea-blue handkerchief and suddenly remembered her dream.

And as she passed the painting of the mermaid hanging outside her room, she looked up and said: 'I'm going to find out about your sewing table, Grandma.'

Mum was quite surprised that Miranda was interested in the table. 'It matters a lot to me because it's full of Grandma's things,' she said.

The sewing table was made of walnut wood. Underneath it hung a pleated silk sea-blue bag for needlework. On top there were small drawers for thimbles and cotton reels and embroidery threads.

The table creaked on its wheels as Mum pulled it over to the bed. Then she opened a drawer and found the key which unlocked it. She slid the bag open. 'There!' she said. 'Now, let's see what we can find. There are lots of shells. Grandma loved shells. Just like you.'

And she pulled out a necklace made of tiny shells and

....

put it around Miranda's neck. 'Grandma made it when she was a girl,' she said.

Then Mum unfolded a sheet of paper. It was a faded painting of three mermaids playing in the waves. 'Can you read the name in the corner? The name of the person who painted it?' she asked.

'Marina, aged 10,' Miranda read. 'Who was Marina?'

'Your grandma of course,' said Mum. 'Marina. It's a sea name. Look, here's one of her diaries. You can read it when you go to sleep. Grandma wasn't very good at keeping up her diary, but she did do it sometimes.'

Snuggled up in bed later, Miranda opened the diary and looked at the round handwriting of her grand-mother as a girl called Marina. The cold had made Miranda very tired and she thought she would read just one page. Mum was right. A lot of them were blank.

The page she read was headed October. In the corners, Marina had drawn tiny mermaids.

'Met the boy again today,' Miranda read. 'He just turns up at my elbow sometimes. He comes from the fisher-men's cottages and wears a fisherman's sweater, but nothing on his feet. His name is William.'

Miranda forgot she was tired and turned a few blank pages to the next writing. 'Horrible storm last night,' she read. 'William and I found driftwood from a fishing boat broken on the rocks. One piece was painted with the name of the boat – *Neptune*. When I dared William to climb up a rock in one of the caves, he stuffed the piece of wood in a hole "to prove I climbed this high".'

Another page. 'Walked round the bay to the cottages and found William on the beach,' Grandma had written all those years ago. 'Looking across you can see my house on top of the cliff. William says he sometimes waves at it. I like that.'

Miranda thought about William and Marina long ago. Then she fell asleep.

'I'm glad you found the sewing table,' said Grandma in her dream that night. 'I see you're wearing my old shell necklace.'

Miranda murmured: 'I'll always wear it. And maybe one day I'll be a mermaid too.'

'Maybe,' said Grandma, the mermaid who was once a girl called Marina. 'Who knows?'

It was the middle of the school holidays and Miranda was strolling on the beach. She glanced up at the tall green house and could just see her bedroom window. Her grandmother had slept in that room as a girl.

Miranda liked everything about the sea. She liked it when it was calm. She liked it when it was foamy-white. She liked the saltiness on her lips when there was a wind blowing off the waves.

She picked up some bladderwrack seaweed, all leath-ery and sandy. Then she sat by a rock, popping the bubbles. She gazed at the sea, which was always moving, always running up the beach and back again.

To and fro went the sea. She had a sandwich in her pocket but she felt too tired to eat it. To and fro. Miranda felt something wet beneath her fingertips. It was the sea, but she wasn't sitting on the beach any more. She was in a small boat, leathery and sandy, drifting out on the tide. She had no paddles. She was just being carried out to sea, her hands trailing in the water over the sides of the boat.

But Miranda wasn't frightened as the waves went to and fro. Somewhere out there she could see a rock, and she could hear something, the most beautiful song she had ever heard. She caught it among the lapping of the waves. Now she could see a figure sitting on the rock. And she knew that was the singer of the song.

Miranda knew somehow that she was safe, because it was Grandma on the rock. The song grew louder as she drifted nearer. She could see Grandma's long, thick hair and she could see her silvery, greeny-grey mermaid's tail glinting in the sunshine. She looked just like the picture outside Miranda's bedroom.

The tall green house on the cliff top was quite small now as Miranda's boat bumped gently against the rock. And Grandma reached out with creamy white arms, which were quite warm, not cold, and lifted her grand-daughter gently from the boat.

'Grandma,' said Miranda, as she sat on the mermaid's

lap and kissed her cheek. And Grandma kissed her and sang her a song.

And Miranda said: 'I've dreamt about you, Grandma.'

And Grandma said: 'I know, Miranda. Many, many times. I like being in your dreams. Sometimes they're as good as real, aren't they?'

Miranda nodded. And she told her grandmother all about her shell house and her bedroom and how she loved the sea. Grandma listened and seemed to know all about her and understand everything.

'You can come and talk to me any time you want, Miranda,' said Grandma. 'I'm very good at keeping secrets, you know. Do you sleep well in my old room? I hope you do.'

Grandma held her and hummed a song and rocked her to and fro, to and fro. Miranda felt warm and happy for a long time. Then she felt a little hungry. She looked down at her lap and there was the piece of leathery, sandy seaweed and her sandwich, all wrapped up. The song was fading over the waves. Miranda was leaning against a rock on the beach. She looked up behind her and she could just see the roof of her house.

She ate her sandwich slowly, thinking about her trip over the waves. It was good to know she could talk to Grandma any time at all. And Miranda wandered back, over the beach and up the steps cut into the high cliff, home.

....

'Mum,' said Miranda the next day. 'Why is Grandma a mermaid?'

They were staring out to sea from Miranda's bedroom window. Miranda's mother looked at her and thought how like Marina's eyes Miranda's were.

'Miranda,' said her mother, 'when I was quite a little girl Grandma became very poorly. She used to say that the nicest thing she could imagine was to walk into the sea and become a mermaid. It would take away all the pain, she said.

'She would sit on the shore while the rest of us played on the sands. One day, my father and I wandered off to look at rockpools, leaving Grandma watching the waves. She wore a sea-blue silk scarf which caught the spring sun.

'A strange thing happened. When we came back, about half an hour later, my mother, your grandmother, had gone. Her scarf lay on the wet sand, just where the waves ran up the beach.

'And my father simply said; "She's walked into the sea. Perhaps she's with the mermaids now. And her pain has gone." There was a strange and beautiful singing in the air.'

Mum stopped talking and looked sadly out to sea again. Miranda held her hand. 'I've heard that singing,' she said.

One morning after a storm Miranda awoke and ran to

her sea window. The sun was watery and spread about the sky. The waves which had fought each other all night were just stirring about now.

After breakfast, Miranda went down to the shore. There was much more seaweed than usual, because the waves had uprooted it and thrown it on the sand.

'It's all calm now,' said a voice. Miranda looked round and saw a boy. He was standing right at her elbow and looking out to sea. He wasn't a tidy boy. His big sweater was rather like Miranda's, but had holes in it. His trousers were playing-out trousers and he had nothing on his feet.

'Aren't your feet cold?' Miranda asked the boy.

'I suppose they are,' he said. 'But I never mind the cold.'

'Where are you from?'

'Oh, over there,' said the boy. He pointed across the bay to a headland where there were some old cottages. Miranda didn't think anyone lived there now because the battering of the sea had made it unsafe. But she couldn't tell exactly where he meant. He could almost have been pointing to the sea itself.

'You look like a girl I used to know,' said the boy. 'She had long dark hair and blue eyes just like yours.'

'They say I look like my grandmother,' said Miranda.

'Then perhaps it was your grandmother I knew,' said the boy.

....

Miranda looked at him. She didn't see how he could have known Grandma as a girl. It was so long ago.

'Where did you say you were from?' she asked again.

'Oh, long ago,' said the boy. He bent down and picked up a purple sea-snail shell and put it in the pocket of his trousers. 'That's the biggest I've ever found. Shall we explore?'

They set off together, sometimes picking up bladder-wrack and popping the bubbles, sometimes looking in rockpools. The boy told her stories of fishing boats and storms, of mermaids and the fishermen who had lived in the cottages.

'But no one lives there now,' said Miranda.

'Ah. Now,' said the boy. 'Now isn't the only time there is, you know. There's long ago, too.'

Long ago. Miranda knew something about long ago. Her grandmother had wandered along this shore when she was a child long ago. And, Miranda thought as she looked again at the boy, long ago fishermen's sons probably didn't wear shoes.

'The girl I knew lived in the tall green house there on the clifftop,' said the boy. 'Do you?'

Miranda nodded. And the boy smiled. 'I thought so,' he said. Miranda smiled too. She liked the boy, wherever he was from.

They scrambled among rocks and climbed up to some caves partway up the cliff.

'The other girl once brought me up here,' said the boy.

'We'd spent the morning collecting driftwood, bits of broken-up boat. And she dared me to climb … where is it? Ah! Right up there!'

He pointed to a crack high in the wall of the cave.

'And to prove I'd done it I shoved one of the pieces of wood in the crack. It had the name of a boat on it.'

The boy climbed up and tugged at something in the crack. 'It's still here!' he called. Out it came, a piece of dirty wood with painted letters. The boy jumped down to Miranda and wiped the wood over with his sleeve.

'*Neptune*,' Miranda read out. She looked at him again. He was about her age. 'Where did you say you were from?' she asked.

'Long ago,' said the boy. 'It's time to go back.'

They walked back and the boy said, 'Would you like the piece of wood?'

'Yes please,' said Miranda. 'I'll keep it for ever.'

'And I will keep my purple shell,' said the boy. 'Goodbye.'

'Goodbye,' said Miranda. And she watched him walk along the beach. Then he disappeared, either round a curve in the coastline or into the sea. She couldn't tell which.

Miranda sat on the beach in her summer dress. Her feet were bare and the sand felt warm on her heels. Around her neck, she wore Grandma's shell necklace. Ahead, she could see the sea going on for ever, until it met the sky.

Did the sky and the sea really meet somewhere, and was that the end of the world? Could you swim that far?

Miranda could swim underwater; she could swim on her front and on her back; she could do practically anything in water and she never felt frightened. She walked into the sea, stopping to watch as the smallest waves ran over her toes. Seaweed wrapped itself round her ankle, but she didn't mind.

Miranda went in up to her waist and her light dress floated around her in a circle on top of the water. As she swam, she thought she could hear her grandmother singing out on the waves. There was no sign of her, just the sound of singing, and it made Miranda feel she could do anything at all in the water.

Then she felt something nudge up against her and tug her dress. A dolphin put its smiling head out of the water and swam beside her for a while. Then another one appeared. Miranda wasn't at all frightened. The dolphins were friendly and she could hear Grandma's singing. The three of them – two dolphins and a girl – dived under the water.

The two fish took it in turns to carry Miranda on their backs beneath the waves in a sort of dolphin dance. At first all she could see was the water and the dolphins, but then her eyes grew used to the light and she saw many different fish swimming by. And still, somewhere in the distance, was Grandma's singing.

A family of seahorses went by, looking for all the world like the pieces that sat on her father's chessboard. She watched their horselike heads and curly tails, only the little fin on their backs working like mad to move them along.

Then one of the dolphins was off and away and the one Miranda was riding followed, right down to the sea bed. They passed lots of brightly coloured fish and a big turtle, paddling its way through the water. Miranda thought it looked rather like her tortoise, only much bigger. All the time she could hear the singing.

Miranda saw an octopus sitting among the rocks. A little way off were some curved pieces of wood, part sunken in the sand of the seabed. She swam off the dolphin's back to explore. A broken-up fishing boat, thought Miranda. And she wasn't surprised when she read the name on one side. *Neptune*, it said. She knew where the piece of painted wood from the other side was: under her bed.

It was her boat, Grandma's boat and the boy from long ago's boat. Once fishermen had sailed in it; now it was home to all sorts of sea creatures. There were starfish and anemones in bright orange, brilliant blue and dull pinky purple. Fish swam in and out of the boat's wooden bones.

Then the dolphins nudged her, and with one at each

side of her, Miranda swam up from the seabed to the top. She felt as if she too were swimming like a fish, as if she had a strong, threshing tail, rather than legs.

They broke through the surface and into the sunny day. Grandma's singing stopped. And Miranda's mother, glancing out at the sea from one of the windows at the top of the tall green house on the high, high cliff, thought she saw three dolphin tails.

As Miranda swam nearer the shore, the two dolphins leapt into the air, nodded at her, and plunged down again. And Miranda walked out of the waves, feeling rather strange to be on land again. Her wet dress clung to her. Looking down at her legs, she thought they looked silvery, shiny, greeny-grey, like a fish's tail. By the time she reached the foot of the steps cut into the cliff, her dress had dried. And Grandma's shell necklace was still around her neck.

the musical box

geraldine kaye

Usually Sophie liked school. She had liked it today until Miss Todd said, 'Oh, do stop dreaming and get on with something, Sophie.' After that Sophie was fed up.

Usually Sophie went to the Four o'Clock Club which Mrs Perry ran in the school hall. The Four o'Clock Club was for children whose parents didn't get home until late. There was orange drink and a biscuit and lots of jumping about. But that day Sophie had her orange drink and then she said, 'I'm going home now. I've got my latchkey.'

'If you're sure, dear,' Mrs Perry said.

Sophie ran across the playground. Dad taught music at a big school and gave piano lessons afterwards, so he was never home before six. But Sophie didn't mind. She had her latchkey and she could always go to Mrs Symes who had *minded* her all day and every day until she was five. Sophie's mother had died when Sophie was small but that was something Dad would never talk about.

Sophie walked along the High Street. Why shouldn't she dream, she thought. She liked dreaming better than anything else. Dreaming was bright colours and whirling and twirling round and round.

At the end of the High Street was a skip full of stuff left over from a jumble sale. Sophie stopped. She saw dolls and raggety teddy bears and a little green box with a gold key. Sophie picked up the green box and opened the lid. A tiny doll stood up on tiptoe with her arms stretched above her head.

'It's a musical box!' Sophie whispered and she tried to turn the gold key but it wouldn't turn. Mrs Symes's son, Billy, was thirteen and good at fixing things. Sophie put the musical box in her school bag and ran to Mrs Symes's house and knocked at the door.

'Hello, my duck,' Mrs Symes said. Behind her were the three-year-old twins she minded now. 'Want to come in?'

'I'm looking for Billy,' Sophie said.

'Round the back,' Mrs Symes said. Sophie walked round.

'Hi, Soph,' Billy said, kneeling by his bike. 'What you want then?'

'I found this in a skip,' Sophie said, taking out the musical box. 'But the key doesn't work.'

'Just needs a bit of oil,' Billy said, dribbling oil into the lock and fidgeting the key. 'Try it now.'

Sophie took the musical box in one hand and turned the key with the other. A tinny little tune began to play, the lid popped up and the tiny doll spun round and round on tiptoe.

'Brilliant!' Sophie said. 'Thanks.'

'Ballet dancer, isn't she?' Billy said. 'Funny that, with your mum being a ballet dancer.'

'Who told you that?' Sophie said.

'My mum, I suppose, my mum knows everything, child-minders always do,' Billy said. 'Colette, your mum was called, she was French. Maybe I shouldn't have told you.'

'Course you should,' Sophie said. 'But it's funny me being half-French when I don't know any French at all.'

'*Oui, ma petite mademoiselle*,' Billy said.

Sophie put the musical box back in her school bag and ran home. Her heart was thumping as she let herself into the flat. She wound the musical box and the tinny little tune began to play and the dancer spun round on her toes with her arms above her head. A ballet dancer, Sophie thought, why had Dad never told her that her mother was a French ballet dancer called Colette? Sophie studied the tiny doll's face. Had her mother looked like that, she wondered.

'You're brilliant,' she whispered. If girls could be called Constance, why couldn't they be called Brilliance. 'I shall call you *Brilliance*,' Sophie said, winding up the box again. This time Sophie spun round herself, whirling and twirling in time to the tune like the dancer.

She forgot about Dad coming home until she heard his key. Then she quickly hid the musical box in her dressing table drawer. Somehow she knew Dad wouldn't like it.

'Hello, Sophie,' Dad said with a hug. 'What have you been up to?'

'Nothing much,' Sophie said.

'All right for some!' Dad said, dropping his case on the sofa. 'I've been rushed off my feet.' Sophie's feet felt a bit *rushed* too. She remembered how fed up she had been.

'I got my spelling wrong and Miss Todd said I should stop dreaming.'

'Poor old you. We'd better have a look at your spelling later on,' Dad said, going to the kitchen. 'Anyway, what's it to be, scrambled egg or scrambled egg?'

'Scrambled egg, I think,' Sophie laughed. Dad liked her to laugh at his jokes. He made the same joke every night only sometimes he said baked beans or baked beans or sausages or sausages.

After supper Dad corrected school books at the sitting room table and Sophie did her homework and then went to bed.

'Bit early, isn't it?' Dad said, kissing her goodnight.

'I'm tired,' Sophie said. When he had gone she got the musical box and played it under the duvet until she fell asleep.

After that Sophie stopped going to the Four o'Clock Club. She went straight home and put on her plimsolls and wound up the musical box.

'Hello, Brilliance,' she said, and they both spun round whirling and twirling to the tinny little tune. But one day the key clicked and wouldn't turn.

Sophie took it round to Billy's house.

'Spring's gone,' Billy said.

'Couldn't you put more oil in?' Sophie said.

'Wouldn't do any good,' Billy said. 'It's broken.'

Sophie walked slowly home. The musical box broken was very sad. Not having a mother was sad too but she had got used to that. But Brilliance was still there and when she got home, Sophie opened the lid and hummed the tinny tune and whirled and twirled and Brilliance watched. Then Sophie hid the musical box in the drawer again. She was sure Dad wouldn't like it.

One day Sophie went a different way home. She left the High Street and walked slowly along a road with big houses and big gardens. It was just beginning to get dark. Cars were parked outside one of the houses and as Sophie walked past she heard a piano. It was playing the same tune as the musical box.

Sophie stopped. The music was coming from a brightly lit basement window just below and she could see bits of black leotard as girls and several boys danced inside. Sophie had never seen a dancing class before and this was a beginners' class with small children doing easy steps. At first she was disappointed that they didn't wear pink and dance on tiptoe like Brilliance. But as well as music she could hear the teacher calling out things like, 'Head up', 'Shoulders back.'

'Head up. Shoulders back,' Sophie whispered to herself.

'Révérence,' the teacher called and the pupils got into a line and the girls curtseyed twice and the boys bowed.

The music had stopped and they ran to the door.
Moments later the class came running and chattering up
the steps and walked off or got into cars with their
mothers and drove away.

Down in the basement bigger girls and one or two
boys, the intermediate class, came in. Sophie slipped
through the gate and ran down the steps. It was dark
now and nobody saw her.

Sophie could see right into the room. She could see the
class in black leotards, the teacher in a floaty blue skirt,
the lady playing the piano and several mothers sitting
near the door. The music was different now and the
pupils were standing by a huge mirror on the other side
of the room. In front of the mirror was a long piece of
wood.

'*Barre* please, everybody, right, first position,' the
teacher called and all the pupils put one hand on the
piece of wood. Outside Sophie put her hand on the
trellis by the wall and tried to do just what they did.

'Straight backs, up and … down. Second position.
Daisy, your head!' the teacher called. She put her hand
on one girl's back. 'Better. Don't lift your heels, Daisy.'

Outside Sophie whispered to herself, 'Don't lift your
heels, Sophie.'

She understood what the teacher said in English but
the teacher spoke in French as well. Sophie didn't
understand at first but she watched what the class did
inside and tried to do exactly the same outside.

....

'All to the corner,' the teacher called. '*Fouettés*.' One by one the pupils spun round to the next corner with a quick little movement of one leg. 'Good, Camilla.'

'*Fouettés*,' Sophie whispered to herself. She liked the word and she spun round moving across the grass towards the back garden. It was like being a bird, Sophie thought, with bright colours whirling and twirling all round her.

A moment later a light went on in the porch and Sophie could read a sign above it, JARDINE SCHOOL OF DANCING. BALLET AND NATIONAL AND MODERN. She pressed back against the trellis as the pupils came running and chattering up the steps with their mothers. Then the piano lady climbed the steps slowly and the porch light went out.

Sophie ran home then.

'Toasted cheese or toasted cheese?' Dad said when he came home a few minutes after. But Sophie forgot to laugh.

'Can't we have sausages?' she said.

'They feel a bit cold,' Dad said, getting them out of the fridge. 'Don't start growing up on me, Soph.'

'Well, I am nearly ten,' Sophie said, humming the musical box tune to herself.

'That's the Sugar Plum Fairy you're humming,' Dad said with a sharp look. 'Where did you hear that?'

'Somewhere or other,' Sophie said.

'Got any homework?' Dad said as they washed up afterwards.

'Course,' Sophie said, settling herself at the sitting room table. 'Sums and spelling.'

'I'll get on with my corrections then,' Dad said settling himself the other side.

'What does "*sauté*" mean?' Sophie asked.

'It's what the French do to potatoes,' Dad said. 'Why?'

'I thought it meant "jump",' Sophie said, but Dad was frowning down at a pile of exercise books and he didn't answer.

After that Sophie walked home past the Jardine School of Dancing every day. Other pupils came to other classes. The top class danced on tiptoe like Brilliance.

Sophie kept her plimsolls in her school bag and put them on as soon as she got to the dancing school. Inside the basement room the class was chattering until Miss Jardine called out.

'Quiet now, everybody. *Barre* please. Into first position.'

Inside the girls and boys ran to the *barre*. They put their heels together and raised one arm and outside Sophie gripped the trellis and did just the same. She was already better than the small pupils in the beginners class and almost as good as the intermediate class. It was hard work with so many steps to learn in one hour and so many new words too. But once the class was finished, Sophie didn't think about it until the next evening.

'Do you know, Sophie, you're not so dreamy as you used to be,' Miss Todd said at school.

But then one day a girl in the intermediate class left the class early and as she ran up the steps, she saw Sophie by the trellis and screamed. The porch light went on and Miss Jardine ran out.

'Who are you and what are you doing here?' she said sharply. Behind her the class crowded to the door.

'I'm Sophie Smith,' Sophie said.

'I saw her last week,' Camilla said. 'She just dances to the music, I thought she was a burglar at first.'

'You'd better come inside, Sophie Smith,' Miss Jardine said. 'The class is nearly over. Sit here and I'll talk to you in a minute. *Enchaînement* now everybody, a sequence of steps,' she went on in a louder voice.

The music began but Sophie couldn't just sit. She got up and did her *enchaînement* in her plimsolls and the others giggled a bit.

'Good girl, Sophie,' Miss Jardine said and the giggling stopped. '*Révérence*,' she added and the class got into line and made two curtseys and so did Sophie.

'Where do you come from, child?' Miss Jardine said as the class finished and the pupils left. 'Does your mother know you're here?'

'I haven't got a mother,' Sophie said. 'She died when I was one and a half. She was a ballet dancer.'

'Ah,' Miss Jardine said softly. 'I understand. So you live with your father?'

'Yes,' Sophie said. 'But he doesn't come home till six o'clock. He teaches music.'

'Music?' Miss Jardine murmured. 'Better and better. Perhaps you could join the intermediate class next term, Sophie. Get ready for the top class and dancing on points when you're twelve.'

'It's not better at all because my dad hates dancing and ballet. He won't even talk about it,' Sophie said and burst into tears. She didn't know why she was crying. She didn't cry much as a rule.

'I'll give you my card with my phone number,' Miss Jardine said. 'Ask your father to ring me.'

Sophie ran home. Dad was home already. He looked worried.

'Wherever have you been, Sophie? Mrs Symes says says she hasn't seen you for weeks.'

'At the Jardine School of Dancing,' Sophie said. 'Here's Miss Jardine's card. She wants you to phone her and she wants me to go to ballet classes.'

'I bet she does,' Dad said, cross now. 'Why didn't you tell me what you were up to, Sophie?'

'Because … why didn't you tell me my mother was French and a ballet dancer called Colette?' Sophie said and burst into tears for the second time that day. 'All I know is bright colours twirling and whirling in a dream.'

'Oh, Sophie,' Dad said gathering her into his arms. 'I wanted to forget it all. The ballet stuff, all the grief.'

....

'But you never told me anything and she was my mum,' Sophie mumbled into his shirt.

'Well, I *will* tell you now,' Dad said. 'Colette was a ballet dancer, right, it was her life. She was dancing with a French group in London when we met and I was a student. But she was an orphan and had grown up in a children's home in Paris. When we had you, she had to give up and her group left and travelled all round the world. But Colette only gave up on the outside, inside she was still dancing. She danced all round the flat with you in her arms, whirling and twirling. Sometimes she danced down the stairs and across the pavement. All she ever wanted was to dance.'

'Like the girl in *Red Shoes*,' Sophie said.

'A bit like that. Then the group came back to Paris and they asked her to go and see them. You were one and a bit when she went just for one night. But she never came back. There was thunder … the plane crashed.'

'Poor you,' Sophie whispered.

'Poor Colette,' Dad said and for a moment they were quiet.

Then Sophie said, 'I went to Mrs Symes after that?'

'Yes,' Dad said.

'You could have told me when I was about six,' Sophie said.

'I wanted to keep you right away from ballet,' Dad said.

'But dancing was always inside me, I remember the

bright colours twirling and whirling and whirling and twirling as Colette danced with me in her arms. Shall I get the supper while you phone Miss Jardine, nearly ten is old enough for frying sausages, isn't it?'

Five minutes later the sausages spat and spluttered in the pan. '*Sauté*,' Sophie said. '*Sauté* means jump in French.'

'You're to join the intermediate class next term,' Dad said after he had phoned. 'You've to have slippers and a leotard.'

'Will they be very expensive?' Sophie said.

'Not too bad,' Dad said. 'Miss Jardine thinks you might win a scholarship. She says ballet's in your blood.'

'What's that?' Dad said when he came to kiss Sophie that night and saw the musical box for the first time.

'I found it in a skip but Billy says the spring's broken.'

'Maybe I can get it fixed in the metal workshop at school,' Dad said and he did. A few days later he brought the musical box home and when Sophie turned the key it played the Sugar Plum Fairy again and Brilliance danced and Sophie told her everything that had happened and she still does.

Nowadays Sophie goes to the Four o'Clock Club on Monday and Wednesday after school and on Tuesday and Thursday she goes to the ballet school in her new black slippers and leotard and Miss Jardine says she's getting on very well indeed. On Friday Dad gets home early and he and Sophie cook supper together.

'Sausage and tomato or sausage and tomato?' Dad says every Friday and Sophie laughs and says, 'Oh, sausage and tomato, please.'

following the sea

karen hayes

Grandad was hobbling along the harbour, heading for the pier. 'Grandad, wait!' Vinnie called.

The old man grinned as Vinnie ran up to him. 'Why Vincent,' he said, 'You'd think you were the old man, not me. What's a big strapping lad like you doing huffin' and puffin' like a stranded sea lion?'

Vinnie felt suddenly important, strutting beside Grandad. He knew deep inside that he was small for an eleven-year-old boy, and scrawny, but Grandad never thought so. When Vinnie was with Grandad, he felt he really was a big strapping lad. Grandad always called Vinnie by his proper name, Vincent, or sometimes Vince. Vinnie had been his sister's baby name for him, and it had stuck.

Vinnie walked tall at Grandad's side as they headed towards the family boat, *Girl Chrissie*, named after his sister. Vinnie knew that boats were usually named after girls, but it didn't seem fair. Chrissie was not only taller than him, and bigger, but she had Grandad's boat named after her. Vinnie cringed, thinking how she could beat him now at arm wrestling, even though she was a whole year younger. How unfair life often was, he thought miserably.

But right now, walking down the pier with Grandad, Vinnie felt just fine. 'Right then, Cap'n?' people called out to the old man as they walked along the stone pier, watching the fishermen sorting their nets. Or, 'How're things, Skipper?'

Vinnie remembered the time when Grandad wasn't able to stop and chat to his mates like he did now, was too busy rushing off to the *Girl Chrissie*, to fish for cod or put out the lobster pots. Now the boat belonged to Vinnie's dad, because Grandad had a heart condition and wasn't allowed out on the sea any more.

Dad was at the *Girl Chrissie* sorting the slimy conger eels he had just brought in. Vinnie's sister was there too, helping him separate the eels and throwing them in bins, getting ready to take them to Newlyn fish market. Trust her to get in there, Vinnie thought.

Dad looked up from the boat, which was tied to the pier, and greeted them cheerfully. Vinnie felt seasick just looking at the way the *Girl Chrissie* rocked in the choppy sea.

'Come on board and help,' Chrissie shouted.

Vinnie made a face at her, but he felt himself go red with anger and embarrassment. Chrissie never got seasick, like he did, and she gloated about it sometimes. She loved the horrid smell of diesel mixed with fish and sea, loved going out in the boat when there was a storm brewing.

Mum was always fighting with Chrissie. 'You can't go out with Dad today, he's going too far out to sea,' she would say sternly.

'But he's going for sole,' Chrissie would talk back. 'He'll need help with the catch.'

'You're too young, Chrissie,' Mum would say.

'And you're a girl,' Vinnie would add. 'Girls can't be fishermen.'

This always made Chrissie fly into a rage. 'Why can't they?' she would shout.

'Because they just can't,' Vinnie would answer, even though he knew this was not a good argument. But all the fishermen in their family, and in the whole village, were men.

Chrissie was calling him again from the boat. 'Well, what are you waiting for? Climb down the ladder and get in and help.'

Vinnie felt tears stinging his eyes but he wouldn't let them fall. He'd have to go down. He couldn't let his baby sister do the work he was meant to do, helping his dad on the boat. But he knew that as soon as he got onto that rolling, rocking boat, he would disgrace himself, be sick all over the side.

Grandad was speaking. 'I need Vincent with me. I've come to the pier to mend some nets for the *Girl Chrissie* and I want his help.'

Vinnie looked up at Grandad gratefully. They began sorting out the blue nets stashed on the edge of the pier. 'You have to do what your heart tells you to in this life,' Grandad said, his stiff fingers unravelling the net. 'For some, the sea is everything. It was for me. Still is.'

Grandad stared past the harbour, out to where the waves were making frothy white foam in the distance. He looked old and sad.

Then he turned to Vinnie. 'You have to love it, Vincent, to work in it. It's not an easy life, fishing. It's not for everyone, and that's just fine. We all have to follow our hearts.'

Vinnie thought about this next day, at school when he was supposed to be reading quietly in English class. Grandad's words had disturbed him. He had known from the time he was little that he had to take Dad's place on the boat, become a fisherman just like all the men in the family for the last hundred years.

Vinnie hated the sea. It was his deep, shameful secret. He hated and feared it. One minute it was calm and blue and friendly, then it turned without warning into something black and turbulent and evil. He would rather be up in the sky, flying a plane, than skipper a fishing boat. Vinnie loved the sky, loved aeroplanes. His room was filled with model planes, and books on great pilots.

But he knew that one day he would have to go to sea. Everyone expected it.

Next week-end was autumn half term, and the weather was unusually warm. The sea was perfect, and Dad was going out again for conger eel.

Vinnie was still too young to be able to help Dad

regularly, but this time the eel were running close in. 'I could use a hand, Vinnie,' Dad said one morning.

'But … but you have Mike,' Vinnie stammered. Mike was the young man who helped Dad on the boat.

'I know, but it would be handy to have someone sort the eel on the boat, so that we can get them quickly to market.'

Chrissie came in while he was saying this. She looked as if she had grown another inch in the night thought Vinnie jealously. Why couldn't he have been born with her sturdy bones and her love of the sea?

'I'll go, I'll go,' Chrissie shouted.

Dad looked displeased. Mum said to Dad, 'Why not? It's a good day, no wind. Just make sure she wears her life jacket.'

Dad was struggling not to show his anger. 'It's Vinnie's place to help on the boat,' he said stubbornly.

Chrissie was furious. 'Just because I'm a girl,' she hissed.

Dad said, 'Vinnie is the eldest. He should go. And yes, he's my son. My only son. I want him to take over the boat when I'm too old, like I took over from Grandad and he from his father.'

Now Mum was getting cross, but she said quietly to Dad, 'You're being old-fashioned. You know Vinnie's not keen. He hasn't the strength for it, either. Chrissie's the strapping one, and the one with the love for the sea, like you and your father. Let her take over one day.'

Though this was what Vinnie wanted, he burned with shame as he heard Mum say those words. He felt like a failure. He should have been the strapping one, the sturdy one.

Chrissie said excitedly, 'I'll get my waterproofs. I'll be ready in a minute.'

'No, *I'm* going.'

Everyone turned to look at Vinnie. 'I want to,' he went on.

Chrissie was arguing and telling him not to be so stupid, but Vinnie didn't care. He'd show them, all of them. Even if he was smaller than his little sister, he could still be a fisherman. Like his dad said, he was the only son. He'd learn to like the sea if it killed him.

At the harbour Grandad was sitting on a bench in the sun, chatting with some other retired fishermen. 'Vincent, my lad, where are you off to?' Grandad asked.

'I'm off helping Dad bring in the conger,' Vinnie replied.

Grandad looked closely at him. 'Do you really want to go, boy?'

Vinnie looked around him. Dad was already climbing down the ladder to the boat. 'I've got to go, Grandad,' Vinnie said.

Grandad sighed. 'Follow your heart, boy,' he said. 'My old one is conking out, so look after yours.' He smiled at Vinnie, but his smile was full of grief.

Once out at sea, Vinnie stopped being seasick. It was a

perfect day, the sun warm and hazy, the sea like glass. The nets were full of eels and while Dad and Mike pulled them in, Vinnie sorted them into bins by size. He kept daydreaming, looking at the sky, wishing he were in the aeroplanes flying high overhead.

'Okay, boy?' Dad asked several times. He looked so pleased to have Vinnie there. It made Vinnie more determined than ever to learn to love the sea, make his dad proud.

But despite the perfect day, Vinnie felt uncomfortable, as he always did in the boat. And though he wouldn't admit it to anyone, he was pleased to be on land when the boat finally steamed back to the harbour.

Chrissie was waiting for them. She was sitting on the edge of the pier, her legs dangling over the side. She looked so forlorn that Vinnie almost felt sorry for her. Then his heart hardened. It was his place to be with Dad, not hers.

'How many times were you sick, then, baby?' Chrissie taunted as they tied up.

'Now don't start,' Dad said mildly. 'Vinnie did okay.' He beamed proudly at his son.

'I bet you couldn't even lift the big congers,' Chrissie hissed at Vinnie, under her breath so Dad wouldn't hear. 'You're such a wimp.'

Vinnie was stung. She never usually teased him about his size. But she was hurt because Dad hadn't let her go out in the boat. Well, Vinnie thought, it serves her right for thinking she could take my place.

Grandad was on the pier too. 'How was the fishing, Vincent?' he asked.

'Okay.'

'But you'd rather have been doing something else. Playing football with your friends, or building one of your model planes.'

It was true, but Vinnie wouldn't admit it.

'Your Dad should take Chrissie out,' Grandad said with a sigh. 'She's the real fisherman.'

Now Vinnie felt hurt. 'What's wrong with *me*?' he said rudely. Luckily Dad was in the engine room of the boat and didn't hear.

'Nothing, lad. You're a fine boy in every way. Your heart's not in the sea. That's nothing to be ashamed of.'

'I want to be like you. And Dad.'

Grandad stared out at the *Girl Chrissie* for a long time. Then he said, 'Be yourself, Vincent. That's more important than anything.'

The rest of the week turned stormy, so Mum wouldn't let Vinnie go out again in the boat. Vinnie was secretly relieved. He was working on a new model aeroplane and was eager to finish it.

Chrissie was irritable, moping around the house. 'I don't know why Mum and Dad won't let me go out on the boat. The fishing is great this week. Did you see all the conger Dad brought in yesterday?'

'It's too rough,' Vinnie said, slotting another intricate piece into his tiny aeroplane. 'You know we're not allowed out when it's rough.'

'I don't see why I can't go,' Chrissie pouted. 'I don't get seasick like you. And I love it when it's stormy.'

Mum came in and interrupted them. 'I wonder if you two would go and see Grandad. He's not been well, and you know he has heart trouble. Take this fish pie I made for him.'

Grandad's tiny house was on a hill not far from the harbour. He lived alone, because Grandma had died many years ago.

The house was damp and chilly. No fire had been lit. Grandad was sitting in his rocking chair, watching the sea through the big window in the sitting room. He looked like he hadn't shaved for days, and his hands trembled as he drank the tea Vinnie made.

'Look at that storm,' Chrissie said. 'It's come up something fierce now.'

'I hope Dad's all right,' Vinnie said worriedly.

'Oh, he'll be fine. The tide's coming in; he'll be back any minute now,' Chrissie said. She never worried about Dad on the boat, not like Vinnie and their Mum did. She was so sure of the sea, convinced it would never harm her or anyone she loved.

Vinnie realized that he felt that way about the sky.

Every time he was unhappy, he looked up at the sky and wished he were there, no matter if it were stormy or dark. He looked out now and longed to be in the air, flying above the clouds where it was safe and still.

He was looking at the sky just like Grandad was looking at the sea, with a fierce longing. 'I should be out there,' Grandad muttered. 'it's not right that they should keep me from the sea.'

Vinnie and Chrissie glanced at each other. They had heard Mum and Dad say that Grandad's mind had been wandering since he took ill, that he talked and mumbled to himself.

'You wouldn't want to be out there in this storm,' Vinnie said. Grandad was getting quite agitated.

'Look,' Chrissie shouted. 'There's the *Girl Chrissie*, coming back to harbour.'

All three peered out of the window, at the scene below. The boat was bobbing up and down like a flimsy plastic toy. Vinnie shuddered, and was glad he wasn't on it.

'Oh, I wish I was on that boat!' Chrissie murmured.

Grandad was staring at the harbour. Vinnie was upset to see tears pouring down the old man's wrinkled cheeks. 'Grandad, sit down, come away from the window,' Vinnie pleaded.

But the old fisherman was lost in another world. 'It's my boat, I should be there. How dare they take the *Girl*

Chrissie out without me? Let me go, Vincent. I'm going out there, where I belong.'

He began struggling with Vinnie. Chrissie had to help hold him. Between the two of them, they managed to calm him down. 'You'd better get Mum,' Chrissie said. 'Quickly. I'll stay here with Grandad.'

Mum came, and called a doctor, who gave Grandad some tablets and said it was his illness making him odd and rambling. But Vinnie knew better. Everyone said Grandad had heart trouble, but Vinnie knew the real problem was that Grandad could no longer follow his once strong heart.

That night the storm blew itself out, and there were stars in the sky. But the sea was still rolling and dark and dangerous.

Mum stayed the night at Grandad's house, but he was so quiet she didn't hear him sneak out of the house. No one saw him creep in the darkness to the harbour, or board the *Girl Chrissie*. The boat was anchored away from the pier that night. Grandad was able to walk out through the knee-high water to the boat, then wait for the tide to come in full and take her to sea.

The lifeboat found the *Girl Chrissie* the next day, drifting aimlessly. Grandad was never found.

They had a memorial service for him a week or so later, at the ancient stone fishermen's chapel on the harbour. All Grandad's old mates were there, retired fishermen like himself.

'He went the way he wanted to,' Vinnie heard one white-bearded fisherman say. 'I sometimes wish I had the courage to do the same.'

Back at the house, Mum, eyes red, made tea and passed out sandwiches and cakes for all the family and friends who had gathered. For the hundredth time, Chrissie asked, 'But what happened to Grandad? The boat was okay. Did he just fall in, or what?'

Dad, also for the hundredth time, answered patiently, 'We'll never know. He was old and confused, his heart was bad. Maybe he had a heart attack standing near the edge of the boat and keeled over the side. Maybe a sudden swell or wave rolled over the boat and swept him away.'

But Vinnie knew. He could hear Grandad saying, as clear as if he were whispering in Vinnie's ear, 'Follow your heart, boy. Like we all must.'

Tears stung Vinnie's eyes, and this time he couldn't help them running over. Dad hugged him gruffly. 'Never mind, lad, we've got work to do. We can't let the *Girl Chrissie* just sit there. We've got to get back to the fishing.'

Vinnie thought of Grandad. He thought about how Grandad had taken his boat out for one last time, and followed his heart to the sea.

'I don't want to go, Dad,' he said, holding his breath as he said it. He knew Dad would think he was being rude and disobedient.

Dad stared at him. Vinnie went on, 'Chrissie can go. She should be the fisherman. She loves the sea, like Grandad did.'

Chrissie looked at him, and it was just like she used to look at him when they were younger. Like her big brother was some kind of a hero. It had all changed when Chrissie grew bigger than him, but it was more than that. It was the sea that had come between them.

Well, Chrissie might still be taller than he was, but Grandad had said he would grow, would one day tower over her. And the way she was staring at him now, with love and gratitude, he felt like a giant already.

Chrissie turned to Dad and said, eyes shining, 'You see, Dad? Vinnie doesn't want to be a fisherman, he never did. I do, I always have. Please, please, please, can I come out with you today?'

Dad looked at Chrissie, at her radiant excited face, and at Vinnie. He thought that Vinnie was growing up, that he suddenly seemed taller, no longer the little boy he used to be.

'All right, Chrissie,' Dad said at last. 'You can come out with me today. Let's see how you get on.'

Chrissie gave Dad a mad wild hug, then another one to Vinnie. 'Get off,' he groaned, shrugging her away. He wasn't going to let a girl creep around him like that. But inside he felt strangely happy, as if he had indeed done something extraordinarily brave.

From his bedroom window Vinnie could see the

harbour. He watched as the *Girl Chrissie* chugged out from the pier towards the open sea. Then he looked up into the clear sky, at a lone aeroplane making a white trail across the deep blue. For a moment he felt he was up there, soaring, looking down on the *Girl Chrissie* as she became smaller and smaller, finally no more than a fleck on the waves as he flew higher and higher over the sea.

someone else's shoes

jean richardson

Why on earth did they have to go to a car boot sale? Especially the weekend Emily was staying with them. Rachel felt sure that Emily's family never ever bought anything secondhand.

'Emily might find it fun,' said Mum, who always ignored the fact that Emily's family were a million times better off than she and Rachel. 'It's amazing the things you find. We haven't come across a work of art yet, but you never know.'

They didn't find a priceless painting this time either, or anything worth buying, apart from a pot of rosemary that Mum said was a bargain at 50p. They'd looked at most of the stalls by the time it began to rain and were making a dash for home, when Rachel saw the shoes.

'Look,' she said to Emily, 'a pair of ballet shoes. What an odd place to see them.'

They were nestling in a cardboard shoe box, and their white satin made them stand out amid the motley ornaments, jugs and glasses, tatty paperbacks and jigsaws with pieces missing that were being hastily shovelled back into the boot of a run-down car. Everything looked worn, cracked, chipped, or stained, apart from the shoes. They looked new.

'I wonder who they belonged to?' said Rachel.

It was raining hard now, and Emily's face was hidden

by the hood of her anorak, but Rachel guessed that she was wrinkling her nose in disgust. 'Ugh!' she said. 'Imagine wearing someone else's shoes. You don't know where they've been.'

But the shoes didn't look as though they'd been anywhere, and Rachel heard herself asking, 'How much are the ballet shoes?'

'Three pounds,' said the woman in charge, who was trying to prevent her stock becoming soaked as well as tatty. 'They're brand new,' she added. 'Never been worn.'

'What size are they?' Rachel wasn't serious about buying them. It was more as though the shoes themselves wanted to be bought.

'Don't know, love. Have a look on the box.' The woman plonked the last paperbacks in the boot, then reached over and handed the shoes to Rachel.

They were her size. What a coincidence. Emily was hopping about pretending she needed to keep warm, and Mum was already far ahead. A hooded figure with her head down against the rain, she was too far away to consult.

'I haven't got three pounds,' Rachel said, preparing to hand the shoes back. She dug into her jeans for the last of her pocket-money. 'I've only got about £2 on me.'

'Your size?' asked the woman. Rachel nodded. 'Well, you'd better have 'em. Seems they was meant for you.' She held out her hand and Rachel counted tens, twenties and a 50p into it. 'Got a real bargain there.'

Rachel wanted to try on the shoes as soon as they got home. Even Emily, who couldn't understand why anyone could be thrilled by a pair of old shoes, agreed that they couldn't have been worn before because both the satin and the soles were spotless. They were a perfect fit too. Rachel's feet slid into them, and when she tried to dance a few steps, it was as though the shoes were taking the lead.

'There you are,' said Mum, when Rachel showed them to her. 'What did I tell you. You never know what you'll find at a boot sale.'

Rachel put the box on the dressing table, and propped it up so that she could see the shoes when she was in bed. The satin had a soft sheen that gleamed in the half-light, and perhaps because the shoes were on her mind, Rachel found herself dreaming about dancing ...

The girl in her dream was older than she was, but Rachel knew at once, as one does in dreams, that it was her. She was living in a cottage with Mum in what seemed to be a large forest, and she was waiting for someone to arrive. The sun was shining, and she felt so happy that she began to dance.

Suddenly, she wasn't alone. A young man came out of a cottage on the other side of the clearing. He wasn't unlike Nick Wilton – a boy two classes above hers at school whom all the girls fancied – but of course it wasn't Nick, because he wouldn't be seen dead wearing tights, or kissing her and asking her to dance.

It was a much more complicated dance than any she'd

learned so far. And she'd not had any experience of being
partnered. Yet it was so easy. She had only to listen to the
music and her feet – or was it her white satin ballet shoes –
seemed to know just what to do. When Nick caught her in his
arms and lifted her high above his head, it seemed the most
natural thing in the world. She felt as though she had wings,
could stand forever on tiptoe, could float, fly …

When she woke up, her thoughts were full of dancing.
It took her a few minutes to remember that she was
Rachel aged eleven and a bit, who didn't live in a forest,
had never done a *pas de deux*, and went to dancing
classes with Emily.

Emily was her best friend although their lives were so
different. Emily's parents had loads of money and were
planning to send Emily to a full-time ballet school.
Rachel had just Mum, who couldn't really afford dancing classes and certainly wouldn't be able to send her to
a ballet school. Rachel would only be able to go on
dancing if she got some kind of scholarship, and there
was no money for the extra coaching Emily was having.
It was all very well for Mum to say, 'If you're good
enough, you'll make it in the end.' Rachel was secretly
afraid that perhaps she wasn't good enough, and she
certainly wouldn't make it without proper training.

She wore the shoes to her next class and was surprised by
the difference they made. So often lately she felt anxious
and tried too hard. Now she found herself relaxing and

even enjoying the exercises at the barre. Her turnout was better, her movements sharper and crisper, her arms – always a weakness – were no longer stiff twigs or limp celery but graceful branches.

Mrs Conley didn't say anything at first, but after several good classes in a row, she stopped Rachel and congratulated her. 'It's all coming together, isn't it,' she said. 'I've watched you working so hard and not quite making it It's so hard to go on practising when you don't feel you're getting anywhere, but then suddenly it clicks. I'm very pleased for you.'

Rachel blushed and smiled. She wondered what Mrs Conley would say if she told her that it was all thanks to her shoes. Probably think she was mad. They couldn't really have that much effect on her, could they?

She was thinking about it in bed that night when she found herself back in the dream forest ...

Once again she was in the cottage with Mum, who was complaining that she spent too much of her time dancing. 'It isn't good for you. You know what happens to girls who spend all their time dancing.' She couldn't imagine Mum really talking to her like that, but her dream mother warned her that if she wasn't careful, she could end up like the ghost girls who haunted the forest and were doomed to go on dancing forever.

Just then, there was a knock at the door. Mum went to see who it was and came back very excited. 'Quick!' she whispered. 'We've got grand company. They want something to drink. Get them some wine.'

Rachel filled a jug with wine and took it outside. She put it on the table and pulled up a couple of rustic chairs before taking a look at the grand company. It was a hunting party from the nearby castle. The women were expensively dressed and at the centre of the group was an older man with a girl who must be his daughter. It was Emily …

Rachel could still see Emily's face when she woke up. She would be the one wearing the jewels, she thought. Trust Emily. She's one of life's princesses.

But she didn't mind, because it didn't really matter what Emily had, as long as Rachel could go on dancing. They were both getting ready for an audition that could mean the beginning of serious preparation as a dancer. If they were chosen, there could be extra classes, a place at a summer course, even – though neither of them admitted to thinking about it – the possibility of a place at the Royal Ballet School.

'Relax,' urged Mrs Conley as she put them through their paces. 'Nobody's expecting you to be Darcey Bussell. What they'll be looking for is juniors who look as though they're enjoying themselves. Rachel's the only one of you who looks as though dancing is a joy. The rest of you look as though you're lining up to be shot.'

There were a few grim smiles, and Rachel tried not to look too pleased with herself. Was it really the shoes? At times she felt as though she must be dreaming, because she could still feel the sense of joy she'd felt when dancing with Nick. She blushed at the thought of him. She'd seen him at assembly and unexpectedly caught his eye. Usually, she'd have been far too shy to smile, but the thought of him in tights made her smile, and then he did too. How's that for confidence, she told herself.

The night before the all-important audition she went to bed early.

'Just do your best,' Mum said. 'You can't do more.'

Rachel was tempted to tell her about the shoes and what a difference they'd made. It was like getting credit for something you knew you hadn't really done. But would Mum believe her? Probably not.

The shoes were in their usual place on her dressing-table. She was always aware of them, even in the dark. They still looked as though no one had worn them, though she'd stopped pointing out this to Emily, who seemed to have forgotten all about them. Would it be cheating, she wondered, if she won a place on a course because she was wearing magic shoes?

She was still thinking about this when she found herself in the forest clearing again …

She was dancing with Nick and was happier than she had ever been. She loved him, and she knew from the way he looked at her and partnered her that he loved her too.

Suddenly someone who looked vaguely like Kevin Wickes, a boy she'd never liked, rushed up and pointed a sword at Nick. Rachel couldn't understand what he was saying. Something about Nick being an impostor. About really being a prince in disguise. But of course he was a prince. He was her prince. Nick was shouting at Kevin when Emily and her father reappeared. They'd been inside the cottage, talking to Mum.

Emily didn't seem surprised to see Nick. She went up to him and kissed him just as though she owned him. Rachel waited for Nick to push her away, to tell her that he loved Rachel, but he didn't. Instead, he just stood there looking down as Kevin told her that Nick was engaged to Emily.

Engaged! Rachel couldn't take it in. How could he be? He was hers. Wasn't he? She was aware of Mum putting her arms round her to comfort her, but there wasn't any comfort. She started to dance the steps she'd first danced when she was happy, but this time they were wild, disjointed, frenzied steps. There was a terrible pain in her chest, but she couldn't stop dancing, not even when Nick took her in his arms and tried to calm her. There was no point in being alive if she couldn't be with Nick …

Rachel could still feel the pain when she opened her eyes. It was mixed up with fears about Emily and the audition, with growing up and the future, with wanting things that were far more complicated than anything she'd wanted before. She was glad when Mum put her head round the door and said it was time to get washed and dressed.

Emily's mother drove them to the audition, but she wasn't allowed to come in and watch.

'All parents in another room,' said a bossy woman who seemed to be in charge. 'We're going to tell you about our plans while the juniors go through their paces. No,' she said firmly, as one mother insisted that Sally-Ann couldn't get changed without her, 'she's got to stand on her own feet.'

Emily and Rachel were hustled away into a changing-room and each given a number to pin on their chest.

'They call out the numbers of the ones they want to stay, so you'll know your fate quite soon,' said a cheerful teacher who was lining everyone up. 'No shoes,' she added, as she saw that Rachel was tying her ribbons. 'Bare feet, please. You won't be asked to do anything very technical, and we do need to see your feet.'

No shoes! Rachel felt her heart leap in protest, but it wasn't the moment to say, 'I must wear my shoes. I can't dance without them.' Beside her Emily, changed and ready to line up, was pinning Number 11 on her chest.

Rachel took off her shoes. Her feet looked small and pale. Were they really a dancer's feet. She'd been given Number 9 and the teacher, rounding up the stragglers, hastily pinned it on her. 'Off you go,' she said. 'Good luck.'

It was impossible to know what the panel were looking for. The audition was more like exercises than dancing. They walked, jogged, swung their arms, jumped up and down, and moved to lots of different rhythms. Then, after what seemed like forever, the panel began to call out the numbers of those they wanted to stay behind.

'Twenty. Seven. Nineteen. Three.' There was no order to it. 'Eleven.' That was Emily. 'Fifteen.' And right at the end, when Rachel had almost given up hope, 'Nine'.

'Of course it's only the first round,' Emily's mother said in the car going home. 'They told us there's only about eighty places for the whole country, so you two may not be lucky in the end.'

But Rachel didn't care. It wasn't the shoes, she told herself. It was me. I did it by myself. And I can do it by myself again.

When she was sorting out her things that evening, Rachel found the shoes in the bottom of her holdall. For the first time she saw that they looked scuffed and worn, and when she tried to slip one on, it wouldn't fit. She tried the other, but it was no use. The shoes were definitely too small. Either they had mysteriously shrunk, or somewhere between yesterday and today Rachel's feet had grown bigger.

She tied the ribbons together and looped them round her dressing-table. 'I shall keep you as a mascot,' she told the shoes, 'because I'm sure you did bring me luck.'

She could still see them from her bed and often thought about dancing before she fell asleep, but there were no more dreams about forest cottages or Nick and Emily. Yet something else did happen.

Later that year, when she and Emily had both got places in the junior summer school, Emily's mother took them to see a ballet at Covent Garden. 'It's a little celebration,' she said, 'because you've both done so well.'

It turned out to be quite a big celebration. Emily's parents had taken a box and they invited some friends to make up a party. Both the girls had new dresses and wore their hair loose with velvet headbands.

They sat on gilt chairs in the front of the box, and Rachel had her first taste of champagne. It wasn't, she decided, as nice as cola, but cola didn't go with this new world of gold and red plush.

She and Emily were so busy looking at the audience through opera glasses, and spying on the players in the orchestra, that they didn't have time to read the programme. All they knew about the ballet was that it was called *Giselle*.

When at last the conductor raised his baton, and the music began and the great red velvet curtains parted, Rachel found herself looking at a forest clearing with two little cottages. And she knew exactly what was going to happen.

Before long, out of one of the cottages ran Giselle, a village girl who was secretly in love with a prince who was disguised as a peasant. Rachel knew all the steps they danced together and danced with them. She was in Giselle's shoes, and she knew just how it felt when the prince – who was even nicer looking than Nick Wilton – took her hand.

Perhaps I read the story before, she told herself in the interval, and just forgot it. But if she had read the story or seen the ballet somewhere, she certainly couldn't remember what happened next.

As she watched for the first time the ghost of Giselle float across the stage and save the life of the man she loved, Rachel made up her mind that one day she would dance the second act too.

dolphin story collections

chosen by **wendy cooling**

1 top secret

stories to keep you guessing by rachel anderson, andrew matthews, jean richardson, leon rosselson, hazel townson and jean ure

2 on the run

stories of growing up by melvin burgess, josephine feeney, alan gibbons, kate petty, chris powling and sue vyner

3 aliens to earth

stories of strange visitors by eric brown, douglas hill, helen johnson, hazel townson and sue welford

4 go for goal

soccer stories by alan brown, alan durant, alan gibbons, michael hardcastle and alan macdonald

5 wild and free

animal stories by rachel anderson, geoffrey malone, elizabeth pewsey, diana pullein-thompson, mary rayner and gordon snell

6 weird and wonderful

stories of the unexpected by richard brassey, john gatehouse, adèle geras, alison leonard, helen mccann and hazel townson

7 timewatch

stories of past and future by stephen bowkett, paul bright, alan macdonald, jean richardson, francesca simon and valerie thame

8 stars in your eyes

stories of hopes and dreams by karen hayes, geraldine kaye, jill parkin, jean richardson and jean ure

9 spine chillers

ghost stories by angela bull, marjorie darke, mal lewis jones, roger stevens, hazel townson and john west

10 bad dreams

horror stories by angela bull, john gatehouse, ann halam, colin pearce, jean richardson and sebastian vince